S O L D I E R S
UNKNOWN

CHAG LOWRY & RAHSAN EKEDAL

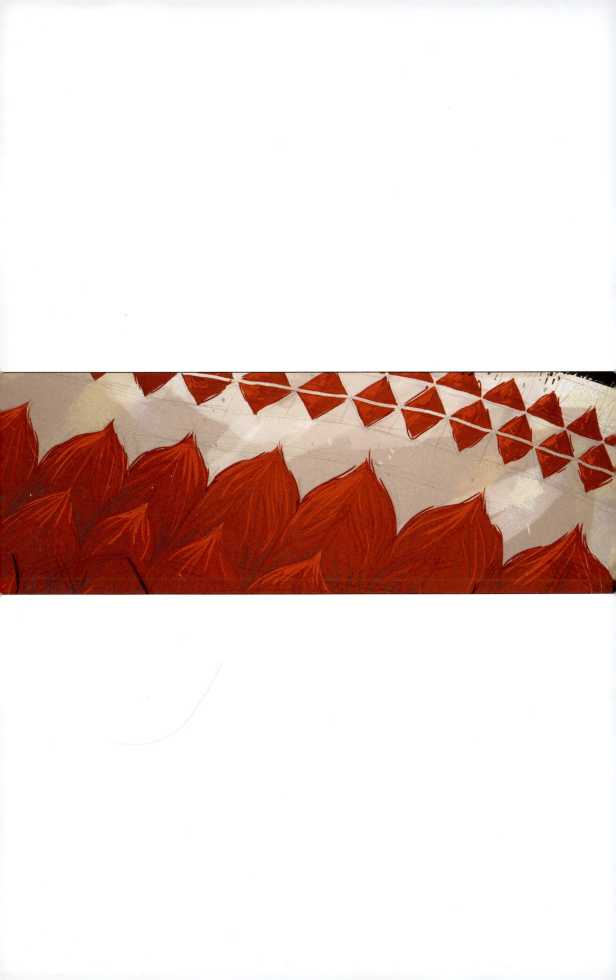

S O L D I E R S
UNKNOWN
CHAG LOWRY & RAHSAN EKEDAL

SOLDIERS UNKNOWN is endorsed
by the United States World War One Centennial Commission &
the American Indian Veterans Association of Southern California.

GREAT OAK PRESS
PECHANGA, CALIFORNIA

SOLDIERS UNKNOWN

Created by
CHAG LOWRY & RAHSAN EKEDAL
Writer   **Artist**

A Larger World Studios
DAVE LANPHEAR & TROY PETERI
Letterers

SHANNON LILLY
Color Assistant

DAVE LANPHEAR
Designer

JAMES GENSAW, SR.
(YUROK/TOLOWA)
Yurok Translator

JOSEF ROTHER
German Translator

Cover art by
RAHSAN EKEDAL

GREAT OAK PRESS
PECHANGA, CALIFORNIA

S O L D I E R S
UNKNOWN
CHAG LOWRY & RAHSAN EKEDAL

Special thanks to Joan Berman, Bold Construction, and the Pechanga Band of Luiseño Indians Tribal Council for their support of this first printing.

ISBN 978-1-942279-28-0 (paperback), ISBN 978-1-942279-29-7 (hardcover), ISBN 978-1-942279-30-3 (ebook).

Printed by Tribal Print Source in the United States of America.

Great Oak Press
P.O. Box 2183
Temecula, California, 92593
www.greatoakpress.com

Library of Congress Control Number: 2019909304

GREAT OAK PRESS
PECHANGA, CALIFORNIA

INTRODUCTION

THIS BOOK IS BASED ON TRUE-LIFE EXPERIENCES of Yurok Native American men from northwestern California during World War One. The characters in this story join the United States Army's 91st Infantry Division and take part in the American military's largest engagement of the Great War. This battle is known as the Meuse-Argonne offensive. It took place in France in the fall of 1918.

The assassination of Archduke Franz Ferdinand in Sarajevo in June of 1914 led to a series of political and military decisions made by countries throughout Europe that quickly led to war. The Allied Powers were comprised of France, Britain, Russia, Belgium, Japan, China, and others. The Central Powers were comprised of Germany, Austria-Hungary, the Ottoman Empire, Bulgaria, and others.

The United States of America entered the Great War on the side of the Allies in April of 1917. The German's sinking of the U.S.S. Lusitania in May of 1915 and the decoding and sharing of Germany's Zimmerman telegram to Mexico in February of 1917 helped compel this action. By this time in the conflict millions of men from both sides had been killed and wounded. During his address to Congress on April 2, 1917 to ask them to declare war on Germany, President Woodrow Wilson stated, "The world must be made safe for democracy."

The American men who fought in the trenches and shattered forests of France may not have known about this grand goal. They were there because their country called them. They encountered horrifying new weapons and lived through unimaginable suffering. More than 115,000 Americans died and over 200,000 were wounded in the fighting. There were Native American men from tribes throughout the United States who fought and died in the war.

They are the Soldiers Unknown.

KEECH 'EE ROO KEE 'NE-CHWEEN-KAH, WEESH-TUE' KEE 'NE-TEY-GER-UE-CHEK' MEHL CHPEY-UE.

RED SYMBOLIZES THE SACRED THAT IS PRESENT IN OUR CULTURE AND THROUGHOUT OUR CEREMONIES.

WE WEAR RED DURING THE JUMP DANCE WHEN WE PRAY FOR PYUEROWOK, FOR BALANCE, ON THIS EARTH.

BALANCE.

YOUR GREAT-GRANDFATHER, HE MADE IT FOR HIS SON TO USE HERE AT PECWAN IN CEREMONY.

DID CHARLEY EVER WEAR IT?

THE YUROK VILLAGE OF PECWAN ALONG THE KLAMATH RIVER. NORTHWESTERN CALIFORNIA. NOW.

THE ELDERS PICKED HIM AND PUT HIM THROUGH TRAINING.

HE WAS JUST A YOUNG BOY.

9

HIS TEACHERS TAUGHT CHARLEY ANCIENT KNOWLEDGE... STORIES OF THE STARS AND THE HEAVENS.

CHARLEY COULD SEE AND FEEL THAT SPIRITUAL PLACE THAT OTHER PEOPLE IN HIS VILLAGE COULD NOT.

THE ELDERS RECOGNIZED THIS RIGHT AWAY.

AS HE GREW UP THEY TRAINED HIM HARD.

OUR PEOPLE COME FROM A CULTURE OF DISCIPLINE.

HE WAS TO BE PHYSICALLY TOUGH AS WELL AS SPIRITUALLY AND EMOTIONALLY STRONG.

CHARLEY WASN'T GIVEN ANYTHING.

HE HAD TO EARN THE RIGHT TO CARRY OUR PEOPLE'S MEDICINE.

THE WAY I UNDERSTAND IT, HE WAS WELL ON HIS WAY TO REACHING THAT ROLE IN HIS COMMUNITY.

HE WAS ALSO ONE OF THE BEST YUROK STICK GAME PLAYERS EVER!

HE COULD RUN, WRESTLE, AND THROW THAT *TOSSEL* LIKE YOU WOULDN'T BELIEVE.

IT'S THE TRUTH IN ALL INDIGENOUS COMMUNITIES THAT NATIVE WOMEN ARE THE ABSOLUTE STRENGTH OF THE CULTURE.

DON'T EVER LET ANYONE TELL YOU OTHERWISE, SON.

I KNOW THAT SOMETIMES, AS MEN, WE HAVE A HARD TIME FINDING GOOD ROLE MODELS.

CHARLEY REPRESENTED THE VERY BEST OF WHAT A NATIVE MAN IS SUPPOSED TO BE ABOUT.

CHARLEY, WHAT'S HAPPENING?

WE'LL BE ALL RIGHT, MOREK.

FELLAS, WE CAME TO GET YOU. THERE'S A TELEGRAM AT THE STORE WITH YOUR NAMES ON IT.

WHAT DOES IT SAY?

IT SEEMS YOUR COUNTRY NEEDS YOU.

18

MOREK! CHARLEY!

MOTHER!

THEY CAN'T TAKE YOU! I WON'T LET THEM!

IT WILL BE ALL RIGHT, SON.

YOU'LL WATCH OVER MOREK, WON'T YOU?

THE BOYS WILL LOOK OUT FOR EACH OTHER.

BUT WE SHOULD GO INSIDE TO TALK.

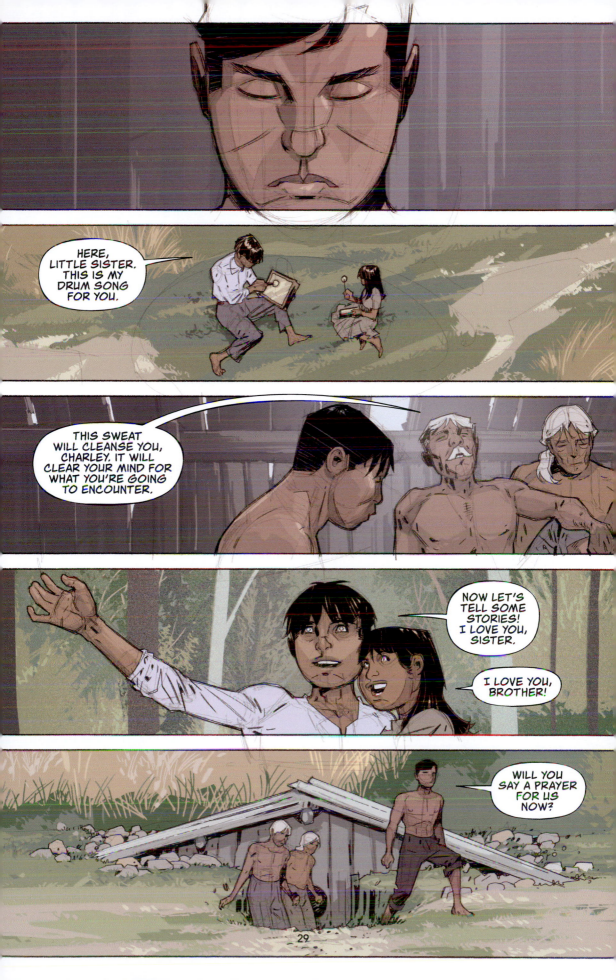

GENERAL JOHN J. PERSHING, COMMANDER OF THE AMERICAN EXPEDITIONARY FORCES.

I THINK YOUR DIVISION IS READY. I HAVE FAITH THAT YOUR OFFICERS WILL ATTACK AND STAY ON THE ATTACK WITH VIGOR. IF THIS IS DONE WE WILL NOT FAIL.

"THE 91ST IS AT THE CENTER OF OUR THRUST BETWEEN THE MEUSE RIVER AND THE ARGONNE FOREST. WHEN OUR OFFICERS SHOW ENERGY AND DRIVE THIS WILL KEEP THE SOLDIERS MOVING FORWARD. I WANT THE MEN TO KNOW THAT WE ARE COUNTING ON THEM, AND THAT THEY HAVE MY FULL CONFIDENCE."

YES SIR, GENERAL PERSHING! WE WILL ATTACK THE GERMANS WITH EVERYTHING WE HAVE, YOU CAN COUNT ON THAT, SIR. OUR MEN ARE READY TO MOVE OUT TOMORROW MORNING.

VERY WELL.

GOOD LUCK TO YOU ALL.

"MAJOR, GET THE MEN FORMED UP AND READY.

"THE 363RD AND 364TH REGIMENT WILL MOVE TOWARD ECLISFONTAINE AND THE 362ND WITH THE 361ST WILL MOVE TOWARD THE TOWN CALLED EPINONVILLE. WE ATTACK AT DAWN."

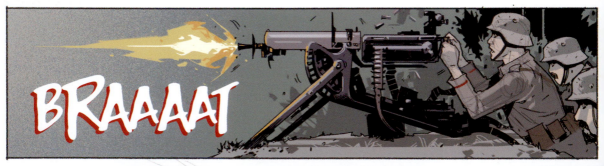

48

CHOOMCHOOMCHOOM

CHOOMCHOOMCHOOMCHOOMCHOOMCHOOM

THIP

THIP THIP

THIP

UHH, UNNH!

DOES HE HAVE A RIFLE? WHAT DO WE DO?

HE'S GOT A GUN, SHOOT HIM!

KRAKT

KRAKT

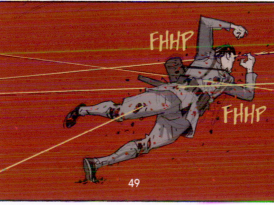

FHHP

FHHP

GOOD JOB, MEN! BACK TO OUR LINE.

LET'S GO!

WHO SAVED US UP THERE?

THAT SOUNDED LIKE OUR MACHINE GUNNERS.

THOMAS WAS UP THERE?

THEY KILLED THE CAPTAIN! THOSE BASTARDS *SHOT* HIM!

WHAT ARE WE GONNA DO?

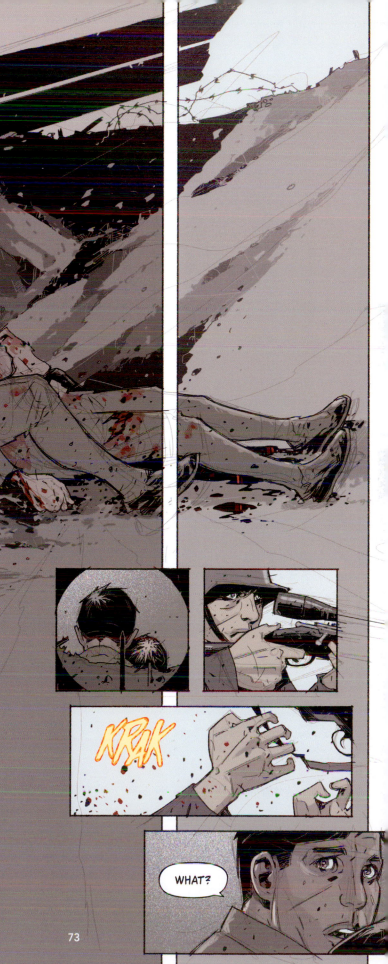

WHO... WHAT ARE YOU?

ASA-SAKA, MY FRIEND.

I'VE BEEN KEEPING GERMAN SNIPERS AWAY FROM YOU ALL MORNING.

MY NAME IS TUCKER. I'M MAIDU, FROM THE MOUNTAINS IN NORTH CALIFORNIA.

IS HE YOUR BROTHER?

HE'S MY MEECHOS, MY COUSIN. I'M CHARLEY.

WHERE ARE YOU FROM, MY FRIEND?

WE...WE ARE PUELEEKLAA, FROM THE VILLAGE OF PECWAN.

BACK HOME WE HAVE CEREMONY FOR THIS. THE BEAR IS WITH US THERE.

HERE, WE ARE IN A MUD HOLE IN FRANCE.

I CAN'T GO BACK TO CEREMONY NOW. NOW THAT I'VE KILLED, I'VE--

WE CAN ALWAYS PRAY.

ALWAYS.

QUIET!

LISTEN UP!

WE'RE *GOING OUT* ON THE LINE! WE NEED TO *TAKE A TOWN,* GENTLEMEN!

I WANT EVERY *MACHINE GUNNER* WE HAVE! WE MOVE IN *20 MINUTES!*

AND WE'RE GOING TO KILL EVERY GERMAN THAT *GETS IN OUR WAY!*

MOVE IT!

WELL, THOMAS, YOU SAID YOU WANTED TO KILL GERMANS.

THAT'S RIGHT.

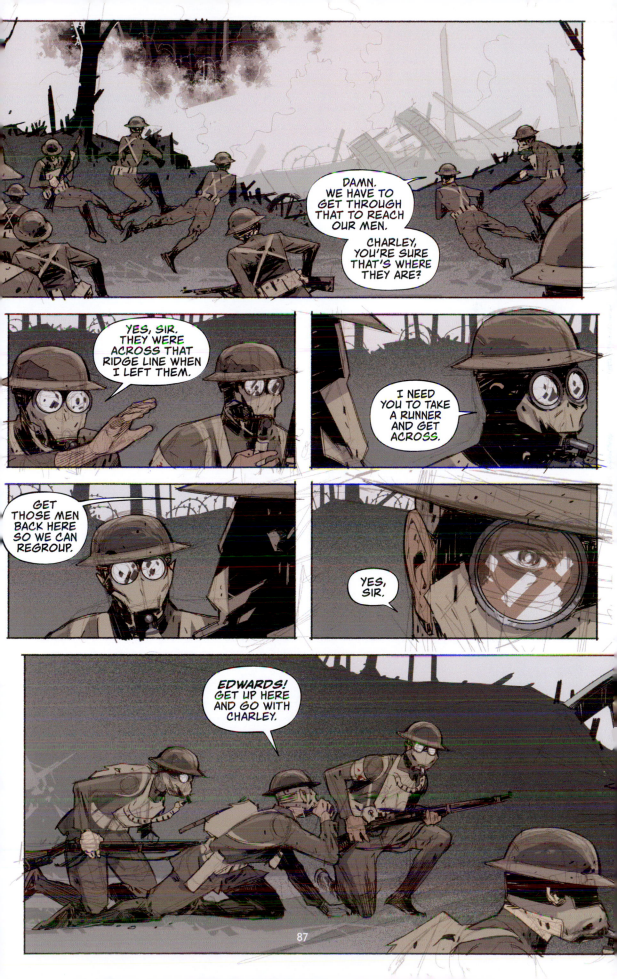

88

KABOOM

HUH.

COME ON, BROTHER. WE NEED TO GET OUT OF HERE.

WALLACE?

YEAH?

TRADE YOU FOR THAT SHOTGUN?

GO TO HELL, THOMAS.

SPLUSH

THAT'S THOMAS!

MEECHOS!

NO, DON'T!

COVER FIRE, NOW!

KRIKT KRIKT

FWOOM!

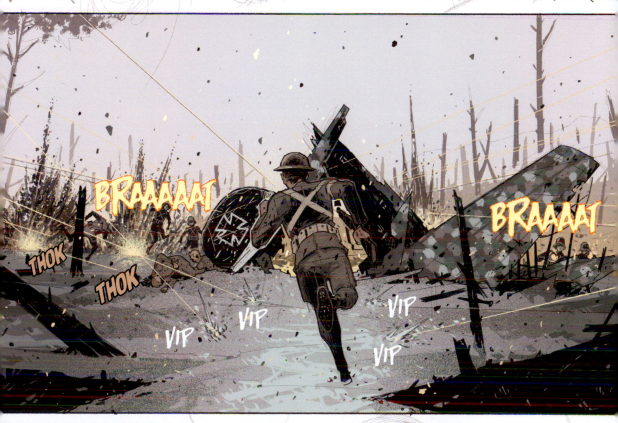

BRAAAAAT

THOK

THOK

VIP VIP

VIP

VIP

BRAAAAT

VIP

VIP

UNNH!

MEECHOS! THOMAS! IT'S ME!

CH..CHARLEY?

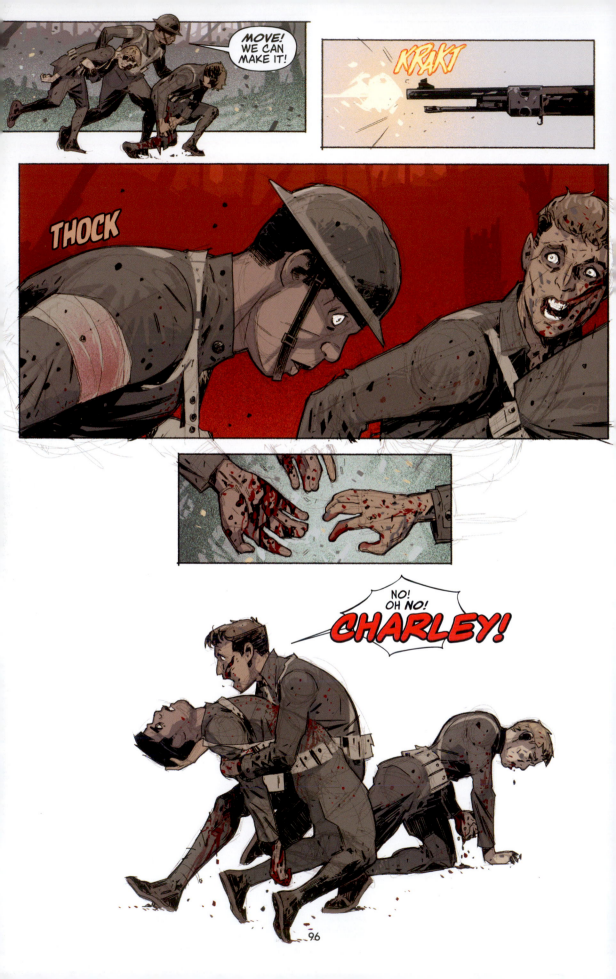

TEMPORARY AID STATION.
91ST INFANTRY DIVISION.

HOW IS HE, DOC?

THE BULLET WENT CLEAR THROUGH. HE'S LUCKY.

HE'LL HAVE A FIGHTING CHANCE.

SO HE'LL MAKE IT? HE'LL LIVE?

UNNH.

HOLD ON.

I ALMOST HAVE THIS IN PLACE.

HOW DID CHARLEY AND THOMAS GET BACK?

WELL, THEY BOTH RECOVERED FROM THEIR WOUNDS AND EVENTUALLY GOT SHIPPED BACK TO THE STATES.

THEY CAME THROUGH THE PRESIDIO IN SAN FRANCISCO TO GET DISCHARGED.

THEN BOTH MEN HITCHHIKED BACK UP HERE TO PECWAN.

I UNDERSTAND THEIR HOMECOMING WAS PRETTY HARD.

FOR ONE, THEY HAD TO FACE MOREK'S FAMILY...

IT'S HARD TO
IMAGINE. WHAT
WOULD THEY SAY
TO HIS PARENTS?
OR TO HIS BABY
SISTER?

THOMAS LOST AN AWFUL LOT, TOO.

HIS FATHER DIED WHILE HE WAS IN THE WAR.

THE WAY I UNDERSTAND IT, THERE WAS A LOT LEFT UNSAID BETWEEN THE TWO OF THEM.

CHARLEY'S SACRIFICE WAS IMMENSE.

HE RETURNED HOME, BUT HE LEFT A BIG PART OF HIMSELF IN THE MUD OF FRANCE.

HOW DO YOU GO BACK TO CEREMONY AFTER WHAT CHARLEY AND THOMAS HAD SEEN AND DONE?

OUR INDIGENOUS LAW SAID THEY COULDN'T DO IT.

TRY AND IMAGINE THE WARRIOR'S STRUGGLE TO RETURN HOME AND REINTEGRATE INTO THEIR FAMILIES AND COMMUNITIES.

THIS WAS THE FIRST TIME ANY OF OUR PEOPLE HAD EVER BEEN IN THAT TYPE OF WAR.

BUT THAT ISN'T FAIR. WHY WOULDN'T THEY BE ABLE TO GET BACK IN THE CEREMONIES? THAT'S WHAT WOULD HAVE HELPED THEM THE MOST!

MEECHOS, OUR LIVES ARE CEREMONY. EVERYTHING WE FEEL, EVERYTHING WE DO... *THAT'S* CEREMONY.

EVERYONE IN OUR CULTURE HAS A PART IN CEREMONY, WHETHER THEY DANCE, OR SING, OR COOK THE FOOD, OR MAKE THE REGALIA, OR ATTEND AND STAND IN SUPPORT AT THE JUMP DANCE.

WE HAVE OTHER CEREMONIES TOO, AND EVERYONE HAS A PLACE AND A ROLE DURING THEM. WHAT MATTERS IS WHAT WE DO TO EARN THOSE RESPONSIBILITIES.

I THINK THAT VETERANS ARE SPECIAL AMONG OUR PEOPLE. I WAS TAUGHT THAT. OUR NATIVE COMMUNITIES BELIEVE THAT.

YOU'RE LOOKING GOOD THERE, WALLACE.

THANK YOU. I'M READY TO SING!

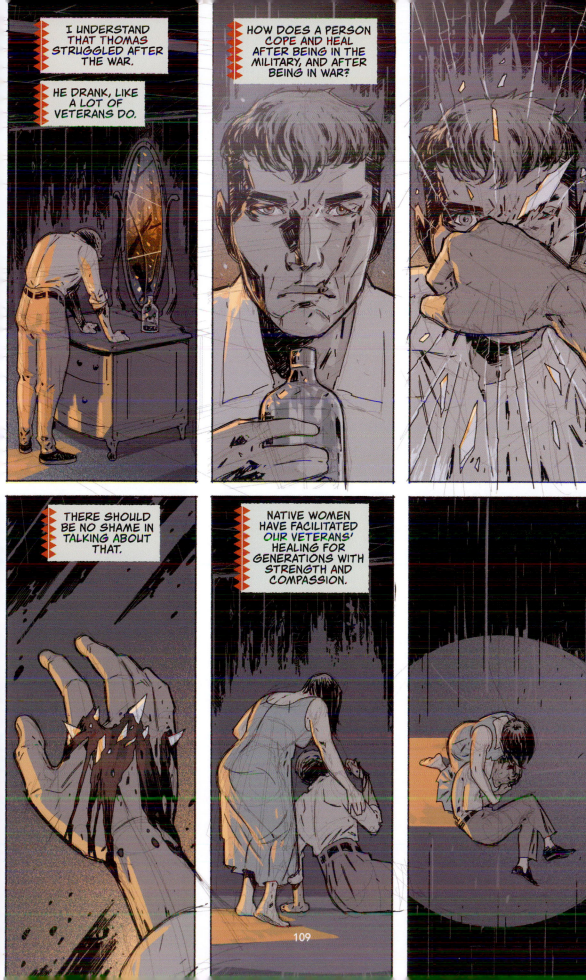

I UNDERSTAND THAT THOMAS STRUGGLED AFTER THE WAR.

HE DRANK, LIKE A LOT OF VETERANS DO.

HOW DOES A PERSON COPE AND HEAL AFTER BEING IN THE MILITARY, AND AFTER BEING IN WAR?

THERE SHOULD BE NO SHAME IN TALKING ABOUT THAT.

NATIVE WOMEN HAVE FACILITATED OUR VETERANS' HEALING FOR GENERATIONS WITH STRENGTH AND COMPASSION.

THOMAS AND HIS WIFE ELIZABETH HAD A FAMILY.

HE WORKED IN THE WOODS FOR A WHILE. THAT'S A HARD JOB. THAT'S REAL WORK.

HE ALWAYS HAD A NAGGING COUGH, THOUGH.

EVENTUALLY THEY FOUND OUT THAT HE'D INHALED GAS DURING THE FIGHTING AND IT DAMAGED HIS LUNGS.

THOMAS S McDANIEL

CALIFORNIA

PVT
US ARMY 91ST DIV

AUG 3 1898
NOV 15 1930

THOMAS DIED YOUNG. THEY COULDN'T FIX HIM. HE WAS A CASUALTY OF WAR.

CHARLEY WAS LOST FOR A WHILE.

HE COULDN'T FIGURE OUT WHAT TO DO IN HIS COMMUNITY OR HIS CULTURE.

HE DID TURN INTO QUITE THE PUBLIC SPEAKER! IMAGINE THAT. HE TRAVELED TO SACRAMENTO TO ADVOCATE FOR NATIVE PEOPLE'S RIGHTS.

CHARLEY WAS PART OF A GROUP OF NATIVE PEOPLE WHO FOUGHT FOR THE INDIAN CITIZENSHIP ACT OF 1924.

CAN YOU BELIEVE IT? NATIVE MEN WHO SERVED WEREN'T EVEN UNITED STATES CITIZENS WHEN THEY FOUGHT IN WORLD WAR ONE.

CHARLEY ALSO ARRANGED FOR MOREK TO COME HOME IN 1921 SO THEY COULD PLACE HIM IN THE FAMILY CEMETERY.

AS FAR AS HIS ROLE IN THE CEREMONIES, CHARLEY KEPT GOING TO THE HIGH COUNTRY TO PRAY ABOUT IT.

HE STAYED TRUE TO THE DISCIPLINE OF THE CULTURE.

THAT'S A GOOD LESSON FOR US TODAY. WE NEED TO STAY DISCIPLINED IN LIFE.

HAVING A ROLE IN CEREMONY SHOULD REFLECT THIS.

CHARLEY HAD STRONG MEDICINE TO HELP HIM. HE HAD THE PHYSICAL RETURN HOME, THAT'S TRUE.

THEN HE HAD TO HAVE THE SPIRITUAL AND THE EMOTIONAL RETURN HOME.

THAT'S THE PART OF THE JOURNEY FOR VETERANS THAT'S OFTEN THE MOST CHALLENGING.

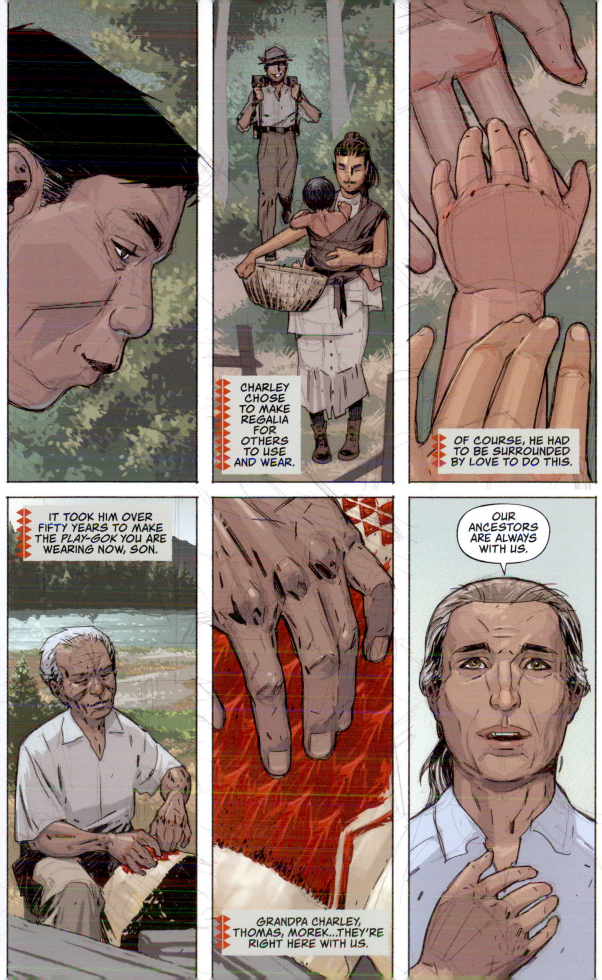

NOW LET US PRAY TOGETHER.

CHYUE KEE
CHWEEN-KAH 'O
WO-NEEK 'WE
LEY-GOO
UE-PYUUE-WEG.

115

AFTERWORD

THE GREAT WAR ENDED with an armistice at 11 A.M. on November 11, 1918. I had two Yurok great-uncles who served and survived in the war. Their names were Thomas Reed and Walter McCovey, Sr. Although this story is fiction, I based it on the experiences I was told of these and other Yurok and Native men from throughout California who enlisted, served, and fought with honor in the United States military.

The 91st Infantry Division was real, and was located in the center of the original American offensive thrust into heavily fortified German positions in the French region between the Meuse River and the Argonne Forest. The "Wild West" division took massive casualties in the first weeks of the fighting. Most Native men from California who were in the Army were in this division. They served as couriers, snipers, and reconnaissance scouts among other roles.

Native Americans were not U.S. citizens during World War One. Despite this fact, Native men across the country signed their draft cards, volunteered to enlist, and served with distinction in the most terrible war imaginable. Native people in California survived government-sponsored genocide from the period of 1848 to the 1870s. The parents and grandparents of the Native men from California who fought in World War One were direct survivors of this state-sponsored killing. This makes their sons' and grandsons' sacrifice unique and poignant.

The report titled *Early California Laws and Policies Related to California Indians* by Kimberly Johnston-Dodds *(California Research Bureau, 2002)* lists monetary amounts paid for the murders of Native people throughout California. This genocide was funded by the United States federal government and by the California state government. This report confirms the oral histories of Native people who have shared their knowledge about this time period for generations.

I recommend the book titled *The Story of the 91st Division* written by the 91st Division Publication Committee *(H.S. Crocker Co., Inc., 1919)* for in-depth information on the division's formation and day-to-day action in the war. The book *To Conquer Hell* by Edward Lengel *(Henry Holt and Company, 2008)* is perhaps the greatest resource for those interested in the American involvement in the Meuse-Argonne battle. It is also an astonishing read. The book *American Indians in World War I: At War and At Home* by Thomas Britton *(University of New Mexico Press, 1998)* provides an overview of Native citizenship issues, the draft, and stories of service among Native communities throughout the United States.

I wrote two books; *The Original Patriots: Northern California Indian Veterans of World War Two (Great Oak Press 2nd Edition, 2019)* and *The Original Patriots: California Indian Veterans of the Korean War (Great Oak Press, 2nd Edition, 2019)* in the early 2000s. The Native men and women I interviewed for these publications are veterans who kindly shared photographs and stories of their family members who served in World War One. These images and histories are what guided the conception of this graphic novel.

The character named Tucker represents the real-life Maidu soldier named Thomas Tucker. Mr. Tucker was a member of Company L, 393rd Infantry Regiment, 91st Infantry Division. He was killed in action during the second day of the Meuse-Argonne offensive on September 28, 1918. Mr. Tucker was the first person from Lassen County in northern California to die in combat in the war. I remember my Maidu grandfather and other Native veterans from that area told me to always remember his name and think about his sacrifice. I chose to work with the very talented Rahsan Ekedal to fulfill that promise I made to remember Thomas Tucker. It was an honor for us to create this book. Chper-werk-see-soh kue 'e-kor-eem.

Chag Lowry, M.Ed.
(Yurok/Maidu/Achumawi)

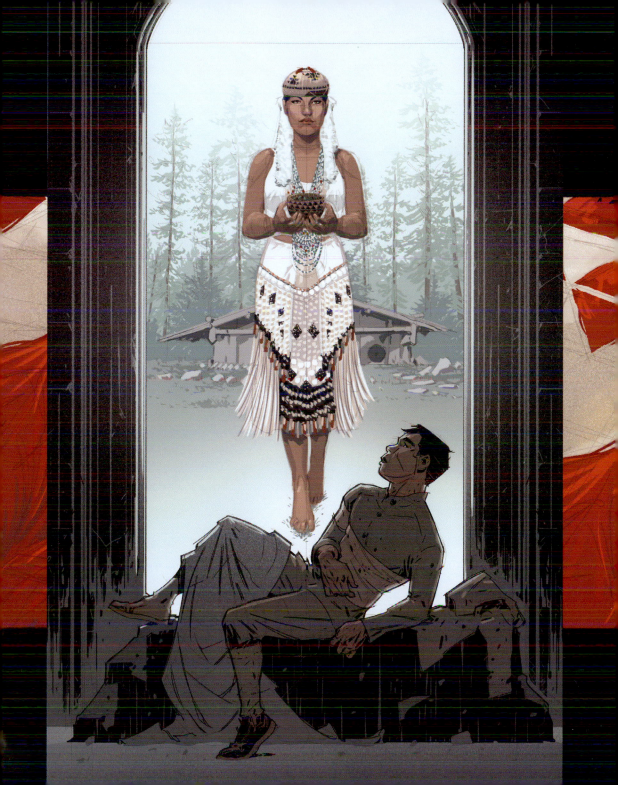